Library of Congress Control Number: 2017954076
ISBN 978-0-06-274133-2

Design by Jeff Shake

17 18 19 20 21 SCP 10 9 8 7 6 5 4 3 2 1

First Edition

The Berenstain Bears®

JUST GRIN AND BEAR IT!

Wisdom from Bear Country

Mike Berenstain

Based on the characters created
by Stan and Jan Berenstain

HARPER

An Imprint of
HarperCollinsPublishers

Does it sometimes seem as if
life is just one big mess?

Is there too much to do
but not enough time?

All you really need is a little
help from your friends.

Of course, life can't always
be a bed of roses.

Sometimes our sandcastles
may get knocked down . . .

or our values may be challenged.

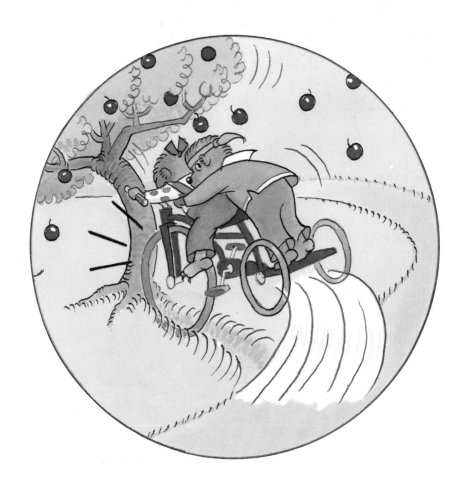

Occasionally, we may run
right off the road . . .

or want to give in.

But don't be discouraged.

This is the time to try a new path . . .

and see new places.

Learn new skills . . .

explore new interests . . .

make new friends ...

or start a new business.

Even when you're down,
remember the good things in life.

Things like

giving a warm bear hug . . .

telling a funny joke . . .

or having a really good belly laugh.

Learn to appreciate the simplest
things in life.

Things like feeding some ducks . . .

saying "hello!" to
butterflies . . .

taking a nice nap . . .

or making mud pies!

Lose your inhibitions.

Start some fireworks!

Maybe it's just time to par-tay.

Unfortunately, the world
is full of sharks . . .

and wolves.

Avoid people who make you

jump through hoops.

Always fight for what you
believe is right ...

and don't hesitate to blow
your own horn.

Use your imagination.

Let yourself dream.

Be true to yourself.

True creativity is always welcomed.

Live on the wild side.

But don't get too carried away—always
keep a firm grasp on reality.

Don't stress and give
yourself a fright!

Some of the time we just
need to grin and bear it . . .

and learn to find the silver linings.

Resist the temptation to zone out with
TV, video games, and the internet.

Beware procrastination.

Never underestimate the
value of hard work.

But take time to enjoy the sunset.

You may make new friends in
the most unexpected places!

Don't hesitate to explore the
dusty attics of your mind.

You never know what you
may find up there.

If something smells weird, be
cautious. Trust your instincts.

Get up and get going!

Let yourself be a bit naughty.

Stay up late.

Create some excitement!

Give it your best shot . . . always.

You may make a big splash.

Try to get a kick out of life.

And don't take yourself too seriously.

Keep cool . . .

and use your head.

There's no use crying over spilt milk . . .

or other such mishaps.

We all experience a few
boo-boos from time to time.

Sometimes we don't even
want to get out of bed.

But get a grip on yourself!

It's the dawn of a new day.

Go out and get involved.

Swing for the bleachers!

Be patriotic.

Cheer for your team.

Comfort the sick.

Find joy in the
smallest things.

Take in the view.

And always remember—
there's no place like home!